Puffin B

Editor: Kaye Webb

Duggie the Digger and
his friends

Duggie the digger was a nice, smartly
painted, self-respecting, hard-working
mechanical digger, until his driver was
hurt one day and Duggie was left alone
to gather cobwebs in a rickety old shed
while the other machines did his share of
their demolition work. Even machines
have their troubles, you see, but like all
the stories in this collection, Duggie's
story has a happy ending.

Michael Prescott is a new writer, with a
special talent for making strange
characters like a fish van, a helicopter
and a vacuum cleaner into likeable heroes
and at the same time explaining the
useful work they do.

To be read aloud to children of four
and over.

Illustrated by Gerry Downes

Puffin Books

MICHAEL PRESCOTT

Duggie the Digger
and his friends

Puffin Books, Penguin Books Ltd,
Harmondsworth, Middlesex, England
Penguin Books, 625 Madison Avenue, New York,
New York 10022, U.S.A.
Penguin Books Australia Ltd, Ringwood, Victoria, Australia
Penguin Books Canada Ltd, 2801 John Street,
Markham, Ontario, Canada L3R 1B4
Penguin Books (N.Z.) Ltd, 182–190 Wairau Road,
Auckland 10, New Zealand

First published 1972
Reprinted 1974, 1976, 1977, 1978, 1980

Made and printed in Great Britain by
Richard Clay (The Chaucer Press) Ltd
Bungay, Suffolk
Set in Monotype Ehrhardt

Contents

Duggie the Digger

ONCE upon a time there lived in the back of a tumbledy-down, crumbledy-up shed in Mr Mudd the builder's yard, a digger whose name was Douglas – or Duggie for short.

I did say that Duggie lived in a builder's yard, but that really wasn't quite true, because Mr Mudd wasn't really a builder. He was a knocker-down and not a putter-up. Whenever there was a house, a shop or a factory which was so old that it was no longer needed or so tottery that people were afraid that it might tumble down with a Wallop! all on its own and hurt someone, Mr Mudd and his workmen went along to knock it down. They put up large notices which said, 'DANGER' and 'MEN AT WORK' in large letters, then they took the buildings apart bit by bit. First, they climbed to the top of the roof, which was a very difficult and dangerous

thing to do. They took off the slates and pulled
down the rafters. They took off the doors and
ripped up the floors and they gradually knocked
down the walls until they were low enough for
Billy Bulldozer to deal with.

Billy Bulldozer growled and grumbled, rumbled
and roared, dug in his strong steel tracks and
8

charged. CRASH! BANG! WALLOP! The walls came tumbling down and Billy backed away, coughing and spluttering and spitting the choky, smothery dust out of his exhaust pipe. Then he

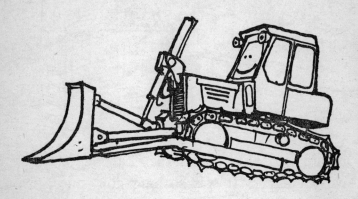

lowered his head, opened his jaws and took an enormous great bite of bricks and plaster which he tossed with a 'THUMP!' into the back of Leonard Lorry. Lennie carried it all away to tip into an old gravel pit which wasn't being used any more.

Billy, Lennie, Mr Mudd and his men all worked very hard until the buildings which nobody wanted were quite gone and the places where they had once stood were neat and tidy and flat as flat could be, but no one came to ask Duggie to help them any more. Before that Duggie had always helped when there was something to knock down; Mr

Mudd had always said that Duggie was a very useful digger. It was so long now since anyone had needed him that Duggie had quite forgotten what rubble and brick dust tasted like, and it was so long since he had bitten out a chunk of rich brown earth that he wondered whether he could remember just how it was done.

Once, Duggie's yellow paint had sparkled and gleamed. Jack, his driver, had always oiled and cleaned him when they had finished knocking down, digging and shovelling up for the day. Jack had wiped all the dust away, covered Duggie's scratches and bruises with fresh yellow paint and taken the sharp pieces of flint, brick and glass from his tyres. These nasty sharp things hurt Duggie horribly as he rolled along the road. Jack had always washed Duggie's mouth with clean, fresh water and then polished his shovel until it shone.

But now, here he sat in his tumbledy-down, crumbledy-up shed, his paintwork thick with dust, his tyres soft and squashy, his shovel rusty and dull. The oil in his sump was thick and muddy and his battery could barely raise a spark. He had a pain in his pistons and an ache in his axles. There could have been no unhappier digger in the whole wide world. But he wasn't lonely.

Mr Robin had made a home for his pretty little wife in Duggie's tool box. Now, Mr and Mrs Robin had five pretty eggs of their very own. A Spindly Spider had spun his web on Duggie's windshield and a family of fieldmice had tucked their nest down beside his left mudguard. Duggie was bored

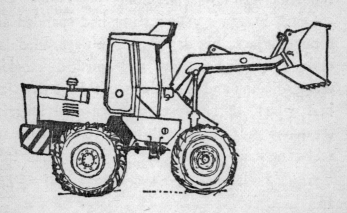

and very miserable because he was not wanted to help with the knocking down and shovelling up.

One morning, just when Duggie was beginning to think that he would have to remain in his tumbledy-down, crumbledy-up shed for ever and ever, something very exciting happened. Somebody – and that somebody was Mr Mudd – opened the doors of the tumbledy-down, crumbledy-up shed and let in the bright spring sunshine and the clean fresh air. Duggie blinked and a ray of sunlight tickled his nose and made him sneeze.

'Atishoo!' he sneezed. 'Aaaa-atishoo! 'tishoo! 'tishoo!'

'Bless you,' said Mr Mudd.

'Thank you,' said Duggie.

'Bless you,' said Mr and Mrs Robin.

'Bless you,' said the fieldmouse family all at once.

'Thank you,' said Duggie three more times.

'Hello, Duggie,' said Mr Mudd.

'Hello, Mr Mudd,' said Duggie.

'It's a long time since I last saw you,' said Mr Mudd.

'A very long time,' said Duggie.

'Indeed,' said Mr Mudd. Then he said something else which Duggie didn't quite hear – or, if he did, he pretended not to have done.

'Sorry!' said Duggie, 'but this is a very tumble-dy-down, crumbledy-up shed and it is also very dirty. I am afraid that my ears are so full of dust that I didn't quite catch that last remark.'

'Oh!' said Mr Mudd. Then he repeated, 'I said, would you like to come out?'

'Would . . . I . . . like . . . to . . . come . . . out?' gasped Duggie slowly. 'Would I just?' and a great big dusty tear rolled down his headlight and fell with a 'plop!' at the feet of Mr Mudd.

'Very well. I'll send Ginger to fetch you out and clean you up,' said Mr Mudd. 'Good morning!'

'Good morning,' said Duggie and Mr Mudd turned and left his knocker-down builder's yard.

Ginger was the boy who worked for Mr Mudd and he teased Duggie all day long. Duggie wasn't very fond of him, but when Ginger walked into the tumbledy-down, crumbledy-up shed that morning, Duggie didn't care how much he would be teased.

'Wotcher, Duggie!' called Ginger.

'Good morning, Ginger,' replied Duggie politely.

'Right then! Let's have you out in the fresh air,'

said Ginger, and he unscrewed Duggie's empty fuel tank and gave him a long drink of diesel oil from a great green can. 'Goodness!' sighed Duggie. 'I've tasted nothing so delicious in my life.'

Ginger climbed into Duggie's cab and tried to start his engine. 'Rrr-rr-rr-oo-ow-ouch!' groaned Duggie. 'RR-rr-oo-oo-chug!'

'Come along!' said Ginger.

'I'm very sorry,' said Duggie, 'but I am doing my very best. I don't suppose that you would be very good at starting if you had been shut up in a tumbledy-down, crumbledy-up shed for years and years!'

'It hasn't been that long,' scoffed Ginger, 'but I expect that it is very hard,' he added kindly. 'Let's have another try, shall we?'

'Yes,' said Duggie. 'Br-rr-rrr-rrrr-rroom!' and, coughing and spluttering, his engine started at last. Slowly, gradually, he felt himself growing stronger and becoming really alive once more.

'Ready?' inquired Ginger.

'I-I think so,' said Duggie, sounding not the least bit sure.

'Just let me brush off this cobweb and away we go!'

'Oh!' said Duggie. 'Do be careful not to

hurt Spindly Spider, he is a very good friend of mine!'

'What a good thing you told me,' said Ginger. 'Would you mind moving into the corner while I clean the window please, Mr Spider?'

'Not at all, Ginger,' said Spindly Spider. 'I shall be happy to oblige. I need a new web anyway.'

So Ginger wiped the dust from the glass and Duggie very, very slowly moved out of his tumble-dy-down, crumbledy-up shed into the bright spring sunshine. My, but it was good to be out in the fresh, clean air again!

When they were outside, Ginger fetched a pail of soapy water and a big clean cloth. 'We'll soon have you clean and shiny again, Duggie,' he said.

'Oh thank you, Ginger,' said Duggie. 'You are very kind.'

'Don't mention it,' said Ginger.

'Just one thing before you start though,' said Duggie. 'Would you please be very careful with my tool box? A family of robins have their nest there. They are very good friends of mine and Mrs Robin has five eggs!'

'Certainly!' said Ginger, peeping into the tool box.

'Good morning, Robins,' said Ginger.

'Good morning, Ginger,' replied the robins.

'Please may I see your eggs?' asked Ginger.

'I am afraid not,' said Mr Robin. 'And would you please not talk quite so loud. Our eggs are not eggs any longer. They are five baby robins now and it is very difficult to get them all off to sleep. But you can peep at them if you like.'

'Thank you,' said Ginger, and told the robins that they had the nicest babies that he had ever seen. He also promised to be very careful and very quiet indeed.

' – And Ginger!' said Duggie. 'Do be careful of the fieldmouse's nest tucked down beside my left mudguard. They are very good friends of mine.'

'Oh!' said Ginger.

The fieldmouse family's nest was a ball of hay, shredded string, chewed wool and rags. Mr Fieldmouse popped out his head.

'Good morning, Ginger,' said Mr Fieldmouse.

'Good morning, Mr Fieldmouse,' Ginger replied.

'This is my wife,' said Mr Fieldmouse, 'And these are our seventeen children.'

Ginger said 'Good morning,' another eighteen times and said that it was the nicest family of fieldmice that he had ever seen. He also promised to be very careful and not disturb their nest.

Then he set to work to wash and polish Duggie and touch up his scratches with fresh bright yellow paint. He polished Duggie's shovel until it shone, pumped up his tyres, changed his oil and greased every one of his joints. Duggie soon became his old self again. He looked and felt really fine. Even the fieldmice had tidied up their nest and it was now a beautifully woven ball with a little round hole for a front door.

Ginger filled Duggie's tank with diesel fuel and left him purring softly to himself while he went away to wash and tidy himself up. When he returned, he was wearing a clean, brown boiler suit and his hair was neatly brushed and parted.

'Ready?' said Ginger.

'Ready?' asked Duggie.

'Yes, ready! Shall we go?'

'Go! Where?'

'To see Jack, of course,' said Ginger.

'To see Jack?'

'Yes! To see Jack. And please don't repeat everything I say,' said Ginger, and he explained to Duggie how Jack had fallen off a ladder when he was painting Mr Mudd's house and had had to stay at home in bed until his back was better. Now it really was better and they were going to see Jack today.

It was good to be out on the road again, to 'toot' at taxis, 'beep' at buses and chatter to the cars.

'Good morning, Constable,' he called to the policeman at the crossroads.

'Good morning, Duggie,' the policeman replied.

Duggie called out to the children and hummed happily to himself as they bowled along. They turned into a tidy little street and stopped outside a neat little house with a yellow front door – exactly the same colour as Duggie himself! 'Toot-toot!' called Duggie and the yellow door opened wide. There stood Jack!

'Good morning, Jack,' said Ginger.

'Good morning, Jack,' said Duggie. 'Are you better?'

'Well I never!' said Jack. 'It's Ginger and Duggie!' and he came out to pat Duggie's bonnet. 'My, my!' he said. 'It's good to see you, Douglas, and looking so smart too!' Then he remembered what Duggie had asked him and said, 'Yes, thank you. I'm quite well again now.'

Then Duggie told how he had been shut up in his tumbledy-down, crumbledy-up shed, how he had grown dusty and rusty, how he had had a pain in his pistons and an ache in his axles, how he had been lonely until the Spindly Spider, the Robins and the Fieldmouse family had all come to live with him and . . . !

But Jack told him to simmer down and take a deep breath because all that was over now and they would be working together again.

Duggie was delighted to hear this. He introduced Jack to the Spindly Spider, the Robins and the Fieldmouse family and Jack said that any very good friends of Duggie's were very good friends of his.

'You-er wouldn't-er care to come out now would you?' asked Duggie timidly.

'I might do just that,' said Jack. 'It so happens that Mr Mudd has found a very old house which nobody wants and it is just around the corner from here.'

Jack's wife made him some very nice sandwiches and filled a large flask with tea, and away they went.

'Why! Here's Duggie,' called Lennie. 'Hello there!'

'Hello, Duggie,' shouted Billy. 'Nice to see you again!'

'Good afternoon, Leonard. Good afternoon,

William,' said Duggie, remembering his manners even though he was excited at seeing all his friends again.

Then Jack and Duggie began work.

What fun they had. 'CHARGE!' whooped Duggie and CRASH! BANG! WALLOP! down went the walls. He took enormous great bites of bricks and plaster and tipped them with a PLONK! on to Lennie's back. He took huge mouthfuls of damp, brown earth and scooped out a most beautiful trench. It was good to be alive!

When Mr Mudd, Jack, Ginger and the others sat down for a meal, a drink and a rest, the fieldmouse family crept out for some scraps of cheese and pieces of crusty bread, the robins hopped down for crumbs and found some juicy, fat, wriggly worms in the soft brown earth which Duggie had bitten out and the Spindly Spider caught a large, plump fly who was foolish enough to fly into Duggie's little cab.

When Duggie arrived home that night he found that Ginger had gone on ahead to sweep out the tumbledy-down, crumbledy-up shed and had left it as neat and as clean as could be.

'Good night, Duggie,' said the Spindly Spider.

'Good night, Duggie,' said the robins.

'Good night, Duggie,' said the fieldmouse family.

'Good night, everybody,' yawned Duggie. 'It's been such a lovely day.'

Then he fell asleep.

Horace the Helicopter

EVERYONE laughed when they wheeled Horace from his hangar and said the rudest and most hurtful things.

'Good gracious!' said Jonathan Jet.

'Goodness!' said Bernard Biplane. 'Whatever is it?'

'I think it's some sort of a mixer – or a fan!' said Arnold Airliner.

'I think not,' said Jonathan. 'Look at that glass bubble thing on the front. It must be a greenhouse on wheels.'

'Or perhaps a giant fish bowl,' suggested Bernard.

'Could be a new kind of vacuum cleaner,' said Arnold, and everybody laughed.

'Hey, you – Thing!' called Bernard rudely. 'What are you supposed to be? You look very queer to us.'

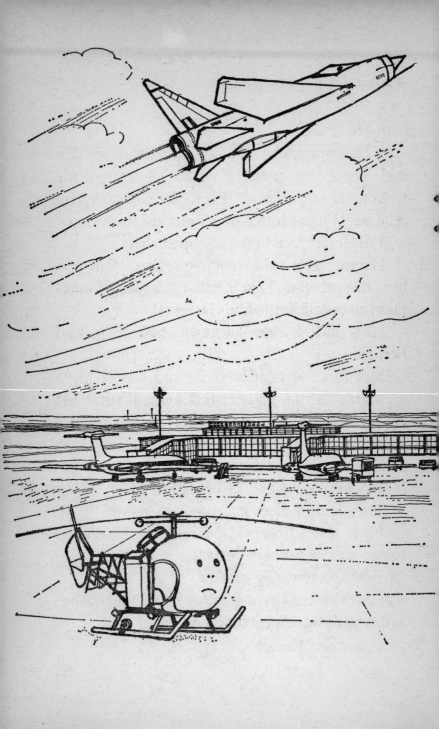

'Please, I'm a Helicopter.'

'A Whaticopter?'

'A Helicopter.'

'A Helicopter, eh? That's what we thought you said. Thank you for telling us, but we are none the wiser now,' said Arnold. 'Let's start all over again, shall we? I'll put it this way – who are you?'

'I'm Horace,' said the Helicopter shyly.

'Horace?' echoed Arnold, giggling. 'Did you hear that, chaps? This Whatsit is called Horace. Did you ever hear the like? Horace!'

'He sounds as ridiculous as he looks,' chuckled Bernard.

Horace felt absolutely awful and almost burst into tears, but he thought that he had better not cry or they would tease him even more, so he bit his lip and tried very hard not to let them see how hurt he was.

'What do you *do*?' asked Jonathan.

'I fly,' said Horace.

'Fly?' laughed Arnold. 'You – fly? That's the best story I've heard in years.'

'I do!' protested Horace.

'How?' asked Bernard. 'You haven't any wings and nobody can fly without wings.'

'I can,' said Horace.

25

'What with?'

'With my rotor.'

'Your what?'

'My rotor – the propeller thing on my back.'

'What? That thin, floppy, bendy effort drooping all over the place?' snorted Arnold. 'And what's that stuck on your tail? A bow?'

'It's not a bow. It's another propeller.'

'Well I never. You are just about the most ridiculous aeroplane that I have ever seen,' said Bernard. 'A glass bubble with wheels, a bow on its tail and a windmill on the top.'

'Extraordinary,' said Jonathan. 'But that's it!' he added gleefully. 'Now we know what he is. He is a windmill. He goes round when the wind blows.'

'Then oughtn't he to be standing up?' asked Bernard. 'The windmills I see always are.'

'He is a windmill lying down having a rest,' scoffed Arnold. 'And he pretended that he was able to fly. Did you ever hear the like?'

'I am not a windmill. I'm a Helicopter,' snapped Horace, who was becoming really cross with all this teasing. 'I can fly. You'll see!' but the three 'planes laughed and laughed.

Later that morning, Arnold had to dash off to America. 'I'll show you how to fly, windmill,' he

roared as he dashed down the runway and climbed high into the air.

'And I will give you a real lesson,' shouted Jonathan as he screamed across the airfield. 'I'm off to do my aerobatics.' Whoosh! he roared and Horace was almost swept off his wheels. He felt quite giddy as Jonathan tumbled, turned and twisted about the sky, flew over the airfield upside down, spun round like a top and finally darted off to play hide and seek in the clouds.

'I am going to London on business,' announced Bernard haughtily, 'but I keep office hours, so I shan't be leaving for a while. I shall show you how to fly gracefully.'

A man in a flying suit and helmet came from the hangar and walked slowly all round Horace, looking very closely at him indeed. 'I suppose that he will say something rude too,' sighed Horace.

But the man did no such thing. He said, 'Hello there. I'm your pilot.'

Horace could scarcely believe his ears. 'I'm pleased to meet you,' he said. 'Do please call me Horace because that is my name.'

'Certainly, Horace,' said the pilot. 'I'm Pete and I'm sure that we shall get along together splendidly.'

'Oh, I do hope so,' said Horace.

'What about a little trip to help us know each other better?' suggested Pete.

'I should like that very much,' said Horace happily.

Pete heaved himself aboard and fastened his safety belt. Bernard was very interested in all this for he was most curious to see what Horace really did.

'Ready, Horace?' called Pete.

'Ready, Pete,' replied Horace, and his rotors began to spin, slowly at first, then faster and faster until they were little more than a blur. 'Away we go!' urged Pete, and Horace leapt into the air and hovered high above the airfield.

Bernard couldn't believe his eyes. 'Well I never,' he gasped, 'He jumps!'

When Arnold returned from America, Jonathan

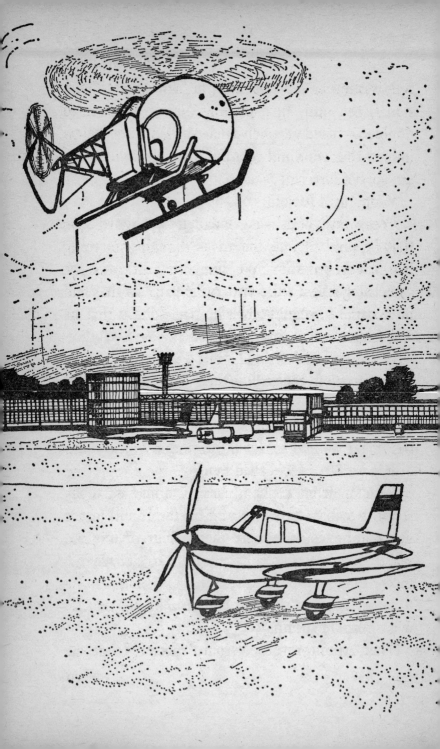

was waiting to tell him what he had seen. 'There was I,' he said, 'just coming out of a beautiful double somersault when what should I see below me but that windmill creature hanging there in the air, sort of hovering.'

'Odd,' said Arnold.

'Yes, most odd,' said Jonathan. 'Bernard says that he jumped into the air as though something had frightened him. We think that he must be something like a balloon to be able to do that and he became so scared when he had done it that he was frightened to come down.'

'Possibly,' said Arnold, 'but I can't see how he can jump up in the air like that.'

Next day, Arnold saw for himself. Pete came to collect Horace and told him that a very special passenger wanted to travel to London quickly, but didn't want to waste time flying to the airport and driving on from there in a car. He wanted to fly straight to his office and land on the roof. Horace said that he would be only too happy to oblige, and when the very special passenger arrived in his motor car Horace and Pete were ready and waiting to leave. Away they went and Arnold saw exactly what Bernard meant.

That evening, when Bernard ambled home, he

asked Arnold if he had 'seen that windmill thing today?'

'Yes, I have,' said Arnold. 'He was frightened by a motor car and jumped straight up into the air. After that, I couldn't see what happened, the sun was in my eyes.'

'I can tell you,' said Bernard. 'I saw him later on.'

'Where?' asked Arnold.

'In London,' said Bernard.

'Goodness! He must have been badly frightened to jump as far as that,' said Arnold, 'but Jonathan thinks that he is really some sort of a balloon because of the way he hangs about in the air.'

'Whatever he is, we have seen the last of him,' said Bernard.

'Why?'

'Because when I saw him he was sitting on a roof, that's why. They'll never get him down from there.'

'Well I never,' said Arnold.

But of course the very next morning there was Horace sitting on the airfield waiting for Pete. 'How did you get back?' asked Arnold, who was most surprised to see him.

'I flew, of course,' said Horace.

'But Bernard said that he saw you in London, sitting on a roof,' protested Arnold.

'He probably did,' said Horace. 'I was!'

Arnold didn't know quite what to think and though he didn't say another word he thought an awful lot.

'A very special job today,' said Pete when he went to collect Horace that morning.

'Will it be exciting?' asked Horace.

'I doubt it, but it's most important,' said Pete.

Horace was delighted to think that he was going to have a useful day and rose high into the air and away over the countryside.

'He's off again,' said Bernard, 'I never knew anyone quite so jumpy.'

Jonathan was doing his spins and turns and exercises again that morning and when he came home for a drink at lunch time, he taxied over to Arnold and Bernard. 'That Horace person is in real trouble this time,' he said. 'I think that we have seen the last of him.'

'Why?' they said. 'Where is he? What's happened now?'

'Well,' said Jonathan, 'he was in the next valley with clouds of smoke pouring from beneath him. He was on fire!'

'He's finished!' said Arnold.

He wasn't, of course. When they saw him next morning, Horace certainly didn't look as though he had been on fire. Far from it. He looked as fresh and as neat as ever. Jonathan was amazed.

'You were on fire yesterday,' he gasped.

'I wasn't,' said Horace.

'You were. I saw you smoking away over the next valley.'

'Oh, that!' said Horace. 'That wasn't smoke. I was just spraying an orchard.'

'Spraying an orchard?' said Bernard. 'What with?'

'Spray,' said Horace.

'Whatever for?' they all asked together.

'To kill grubs and flies and caterpillars – pests like that,' said Horace.

'My word,' said Arnold. 'That just about takes the biscuit. He's an airborne fly-spray!'

'I'm confused,' said Bernard.

Jonathan was a very puzzled jet when he set off for his daily exercises that morning. 'I can't make it out,' he said to himself.

Shortly after dinner, Pete and another airman drove across the airfield at a terrific speed. They shot beneath Arnold and under Bernard's nose and stopped beside Horace with a screech of brakes and a cloud of dust.

'Emergency!' shouted Pete. 'Get going, Horace!' and Horace shot into the air like a cork from a bottle. Pete told Horace to head out to sea and to keep his eyes open. He didn't say what to look for, but Horace didn't really need to be told. He knew he must look for something unusual and he soon saw it. 'There is a tiny orange boat in the water down there, Pete,' he said, 'and the man in it is waving.'

'Good lad!' said Pete. 'Hover low over his head, Horace. We are going to pick him up.' Horace did as he was told. 'Hold steady, Horace,' called Pete. 'We are lowering him a rope. Be ready to take the strain and the extra weight when we haul him up!'

'Right!' replied Horace, and in a few moments the airman – for that is what he was – was hauled to safety in Horace's cabin and Pete was saying, 'Hospital, Horace! Fast as you can!' When they reached the hospital, Horace landed on the lawn and the airman was carried indoors.

While Horace was busy dealing with his emergency, Bernard saw Jonathan coming in to land and noticed that something was wrong. 'Look out, Arnold!' he shouted. 'Here comes Jonathan. He

must have been taken ill. He sounds awful and can hardly hold up his wings.' Jonathan landed heavily, his engine gasped and spluttered and he let out a long, low moan. 'I feel dreadful,' he said.

'Whatever's wrong?' asked Arnold. 'You look terrible. Are you ill?'

'It's much worse than that.'

'Worse?'

'Yes, I believe that I sprained something when I looped the loop and my pilot thought that we should crash.'

'How awful,' said Bernard.

'But that's not the worst,' groaned Jonathan. 'My pilot ordered my observer to bale out and he parachuted into the sea. It was awful. He'll be drowned and I shall get the blame.'

'No you won't,' said Horace, who had arrived unnoticed while they talked. 'Your observer is quite safe, but he'll be in hospital for a day or two. He was very cold and wet.'

'What do *you* know about it?' snorted Jonathan. 'He was *my* observer.'

But before Horace could reply, Pete wanted him again. 'Where to this time?' asked Horace.

'To church,' said Pete.

'Me, at church?' spluttered Horace with great

38

surprise. 'Whatever for? How can I go to church?'

'You'll see!' said Pete mysteriously.

Shortly after Horace had left, Bernard went off on a local trip and saw something so extraordinary, he couldn't get back fast enough to tell the others.

'He's really done it now,' he gasped breathlessly as he landed.

'Who has?' asked Arnold and Jonathan.

'Old Thingummy-whiz! Who else?'

'Do you mean Horace Helicopter?' asked Jonathan. 'Because if you do, use his name. He has one.'

'You've changed your tune,' snapped Bernard.

'With very good reason,' replied Jonathan sternly. 'But suppose you tell us what you think Horace has done.'

'I don't *think* he's done anything. I *know*!' growled Bernard. 'He has stolen the weather-vane from the new church in the big town,' he went on. 'I saw him with it. It was dangling underneath him for everyone to see. He's a thief!'

'I don't believe that!' said Arnold.

'Nor do I,' said Jonathan. 'And I hope that you'll apologize to him when he comes home. That was a horrid thing to say!'

'One would think that he was a friend of yours,' sneered Bernard.

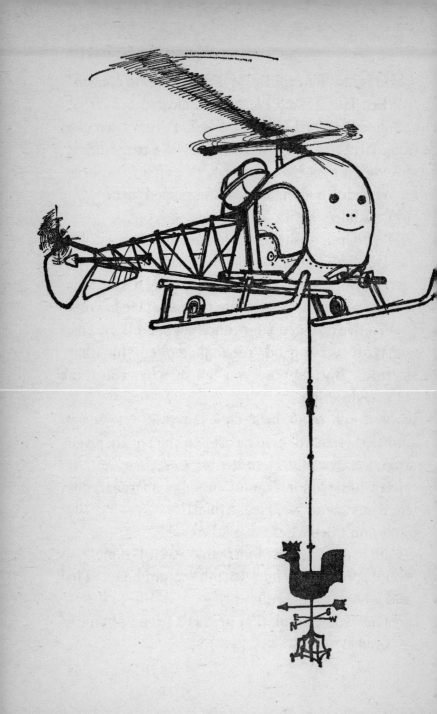

'He is,' said Arnold. 'Be quiet. Here he comes!'

When Horace landed, Arnold cleared his throat and said, 'Hello, Horace. We are sorry that we were so rude and unkind to you. We won't do it again.'

'We didn't understand you,' said Jonathan.

'You didn't even try,' said Pete severely.

'That's all right, Pete,' said Horace. 'I don't mind now. Let's forget all about it and be friends.'

'Be friends by all means,' said Pete. 'But I believe that these three aeroplanes should first be taught something about helicopters and their work.'

'Yes, do tell us,' they begged. 'Tell us how it is that you can manage to jump straight up into the air and stay there.'

'Well . . .' began Horace.

'You rest. I'll tell them!' ordered Pete. 'If you tell them about yourself, you'll leave out all the important things.'

Pete leaned against Horace and began. 'Horace isn't large and powerful like you Arnold,' he said, 'and he can't fly all the way to America with lots of passengers on board.'

''Course not!' scoffed Horace.

'Be quiet!' said Pete, and then went on, 'Horace isn't a comfortable private plane who carries business men around like Bernard.'

'He does carry passengers though,' said Arnold.

'Sometimes,' agreed Pete. 'But neither is Horace a very tough, fast war-plane, ready and able to protect us like Jonathan.'

'No,' said Horace. 'I am a helicopter.'

'Exactly,' said Pete. 'And Horace doesn't need a great airfield and runway to take off like you three. He can fly up or down, backwards or forwards and even sideways if he likes. Or he can just hover and hang in the air.'

'So when I saw him on that roof in London he had landed there on purpose – quite deliberately,' said Bernard.

'Of course,' said Pete. 'We took a very special passenger straight to his office. We landed on the roof and he simply had to walk downstairs.'

'Well I never!' said Arnold.

'So that was how you were able to pull my observer out of the sea,' said Jonathan. 'You hovered!'

'Yes,' said Horace. 'And we landed on the hospital lawn.'

'Goodness me,' said Bernard. 'Then I don't

suppose that you were stealing the church weather-cock.'

Pete and Horace roared with laughter. 'You silly old biplane,' chuckled Pete. 'We were lifting it to the top of the church steeple for the workmen to fix. It's much easier for them if we do that.'

'Well!' they all said.

So Horace became the friend of everyone at the airfield and of many others besides. He helped Libbie Lifeboat whenever she needed assistance. He helped the police and the fire service. He helped the farmers, he helped build factories and carry power cables across valleys. He flew very sick people to hospital and took special medicines where they were needed. He helped take photo-graphs and do all sorts of other useful things, in fact he was the busiest little fellow on the airfield. No one dares say a single thing against Horace these days or they would have Jonathan Jet to deal with too.

Freddie the Fish Van

FREDDIE was drawn slowly and gently from the workshop where he had just been made and out into the sunshine for the very first time. He was not yet used to his wheels and felt just a little bit wobbly on them. His couplings were stiff and they creaked as they stretched and tightened and there seemed to be some fluff in his brake-pipes which was jiggling back and forth and tickling his tummy. All this was new and exciting and very strange indeed.

Suddenly there was a sharp 'Peep!' from somewhere in front of him. Freddie almost jumped off his axles with fright. 'Whatever was that?' he gasped.

'Peep!' There it was again and Freddie felt his buffers touch those of his companions before and behind him. Now they moved even more slowly and gently, and he felt his wheels bumping over gaps in the rails beneath them. 'Chunk-chunk!' they went. 'Chunk-chunk!'

'Oh!' said Freddie. 'The road is broken up,' and for a moment he felt a little scared. But he breathed

easier as his couplings tightened and as he was drawn forward a little more quickly he felt his wheels on straight, unbroken track one more. A few moments later, Freddie's brakes tightened, his buffers were gently squashed against those of his companions and he stopped.

Freddie relaxed and rested on trembling wheels.

'Where are we?' asked someone.

'I've no idea,' said Freddie.

'It wouldn't help much if we knew,' said somebody else. 'We don't know anything about anything yet.'

'True,' said Freddie as he looked about him. It was all very strange.

All that day, Freddie and his friends stood where they had been left and when it grew dark he fell into a deep and dreamless sleep. Next morning, he was awakened by a man with a very loud voice, who said, 'Pay attention everyone! Today, you begin your training.' Freddie was excited and listened very carefully. 'You will be told everything you should know and taught your job thoroughly,' said the man. 'When you leave here to go to your owners you will be fully trained railway vans and waggons.' Then he added, 'I am the Yard Foreman and this,' he said, pointing to a little green diesel who stood beside him, 'will be your teacher – Sammy Shunter!'

'So that's what we are,' thought Freddie. 'Railway waggons and vans!'

'Toot!' said Sammy. 'Today, I shall teach you how to form trains.'

Freddie and his friends were pulled and pushed about all over the sidings and were taught to cross points properly, how to link couplings and how to be shunted. Sammy pushed them faster and faster over the tracks, and then stopped suddenly. This was a little alarming at first and an awful strain on the couplings. Then the foreman unfastened Freddie and said, 'Your turn now!' Freddie felt himself pushed quickly up the track and then Sammy stopped. Freddie didn't! He went on all by himself.

'Oh, oh!' he said when he realized what was happening and then, when he had overcome his surprise, he began to enjoy it. 'Whee-ee-ee!' he shouted as he trundled over the track, until he noticed that there was another van and several trucks in front of him, but they were standing quite still.

'Look out!' he shouted. He closed his eyes and – 'CLUNK!' His buffers hit those of the other van and were squashed back on their springs. 'Oof!' gasped Freddie, and stopped. So this was what shunting was about!

For the next few days, Sammy and the foreman worked them very hard. They shunted and formed trains. They were pulled and pushed with unconnected vacuum brakes which rattled and banged them about quite a lot. Then they were run quickly and taught how to apply their brakes smoothly and correctly, which was much better. They also met a brake van who followed them wherever they went and made quite certain that they didn't mess about when Sammy wasn't looking their way.

On their last day at Training School, Sammy took them all for a brisk run on the main line. This was the most exciting day of all, but everyone was very frightened when an express train rushed past them with a rattle and a roar which left them all quite deaf and dizzy. 'You will soon become used to that,' said Sammy kindly as he took them back to the yard.

Next day, the foreman gathered them all together and said, 'I am delighted to tell you that you have all passed your examinations with flying colours and are now fully trained waggons and vans.'

'Hooray!' they shouted.

'Today,' continued the foreman, 'A big diesel will collect you and deliver you to your owners.'

They were all sorry to hear that they would soon be leaving Sammy, the foreman and their home in the works yard, but they were all very excited too and wondered where they would be going. More important, they wondered what their owners would be like.

Later that morning, Sammy shunted them and made them form trains for the last time and a strange and very severe brake van was coupled behind Freddie, who was last in the line.

The foreman came into the yard.

'A-ten-shun!' snapped the brake van. 'Stand by for inspection!'

The foreman walked slowly down the line look-ing closely at everyone and nodding in a satisfied sort of way. An enormous diesel purred into the yard and backed down on them. He was coupled to this train of smart new waggons and vans. Freddie felt his brakes ease and his couplings tighten. 'Take them away, Diesel!' shouted the foreman, 'Good-bye, everyone.'

'Good-bye, Mr Foreman!' they shouted. 'Good-bye, Sammy!'

'Peep!' said Sammy sadly, sorry to see them go.

Out on the main line, Diesel's purr changed to a powerful roar and they flew along so fast that their wheels seemed hardly to touch the track. The speed was so exciting that it almost took their breath away as they flashed past fields and houses, farms and factories. They roared through stations and over roads and rivers. Tunnels were a little 'scarey' at first, but they soon became used to them, though one was so long that Freddie began to wonder if they would ever see daylight again.

At last, they slowed down and stopped beside great, black hills. Two huge wheels reared into the

air and chimneys belched clouds of smoke and steam. Hundreds of trucks stood in long, grey ranks on the sidings. A colliery! Diesel moved forward and a rough, grimy shunter bustled up and took off the new trucks. Diesel backed down on the train again and they were off once more. They stopped at an oil refinery to leave the oil tankers. Several vans were delivered to a factory and more were left on a busy siding in a large town through which they passed. Only Freddie and Brake Van remained and they went on and on, until Brake Van said, 'Here we are – the end of the line!'

'Where's that?' asked Freddie.

'Here,' said Brake Van.

'What's here?'

'The harbour, of course.'

When Diesel had gone, Freddie looked about him. 'That must be the sea,' he said to himself. 'I've heard about that. And those things there must be ships.'

'Fishing boats, actually!' said a voice from the next track. 'I'm Fergus. I've worked here for ages.'

'Hello, Fergus,' said Freddie and introduced himself.

Fergus was a large white van, just like Freddie.

When Freddie awoke next morning, he looked

for Fergus, but Fergus had been taken away overnight. Freddie felt very lonely indeed, but brightened up a little when a railwayman and a gentleman in a spotless white coat came up to speak to him. 'Good afternoon,' said White Coat. 'I am your owner.' Then, turning to the railwayman, he added, 'And this is the Yard Master.'

'Good afternoon,' replied Freddie. 'I'm very pleased to meet you.' The owner and the Yard Master looked very carefully at Freddie, they peered beneath him, opened his doors and stomped about inside him.

'Very nice,' said the owner. 'First class,' and they both went away again.

As they left, a small diesel brought a long train into the yard and he was followed by another engine with an even longer train. 'Now I shall have company,' thought Freddie. A fussy blue shunter chattered into the yard and began to sort out the other trucks and waggons.

A yellow van came rumbling towards Freddie and gave him an awful bang. 'Ouch!' he said. But the yellow van didn't apologize. All he said was 'Pooh! Don't breathe all over me. I am a banana van.'

Before Freddie could reply he was whisked away

and sent careering towards a large silver tank waggon. The tanker saw Freddie coming and shouted, 'Keep him away from me! I am a petrol tanker!'

Freddie was becoming quite upset by all this. A row of coal waggons were even ruder. 'Don't come near us,' they said. 'We don't want your sort touching us!' A cattle truck full of pigs screamed, 'Get away from me you horrid thing. You will upset my passengers.' A milk tanker was absolutely furious to find himself next to Freddie. 'Phew!' he said, 'I don't want you near me. Your smell will turn my milk sour!'

Freddie was so unhappy that he was almost in tears. 'What *is* wrong with me?' he asked.

Milk Tanker sniffed and said, 'If *you* don't know then I'm sorry for you. You must be the only van without a sense of smell, but I suppose that you are used to it. I'm not!'

Once more, Freddie found himself standing alone, until, just as it grew dark, the little blue shunter bustled into the yard and chuttered up to Freddie. 'Come along, young man,' he said kindly but firmly to Freddie. 'Your friends are waiting for you. You can't spend your life here in the middle of a siding.'

'I don't have any friends,' said Freddie. 'None of the others like me. They treat me as though – as though – I smelt!'

Blue Shunter chuckled. 'I thought as much,' he said.

'I don't think it's at all funny,' moaned Freddie. 'And I don't smell except of new paint!'

'Of course you don't – and won't!' soothed Blue Shunter. 'But you are a fish van you know and the others always say that you do!'

'Why?' demanded Freddie.

'Your people used to smell awful when my grandfather was a young engine,' replied Blue Shunter, 'and I must admit that stale fish isn't a favourite smell of mine. But now, you are all refrigerated steel vans and the "XP" on your sides means that you can all be used to form "Fish Specials". You can keep the fish frozen and fresh while you whisk it straight from the trawlers at the quayside to the markets in the big cities.'

'Then we are very useful and important,' said Freddie.

'Indeed you are,' said Blue Shunter. 'Now get along and join your friends!' and he stopped suddenly and sent Freddie scuttling down the track to join a train of shiny white fish vans.

'Clunk!' Freddie felt someone shaking him by the buffer.

'Hello!' said a voice which he knew.

'Fergus!' cried Freddie happily. 'Hello!'

'Welcome to the family!' chorused the others.

Boxes of fish were lifted from the holds of the trawlers by long groping cranes and set down on the quay. Busy forklifts loaded the boxes into the train of vans and Freddie was filled with boxes of cod and skate, hake and herring, plaice, mackerel and mullet. All the doors were slammed and sealed tight and, gasping and grunting, wheezing and whistling, Blue Shunter hauled them to the main line. There, a huge electric locomotive waited to pull them away.

When the couplings had been made, the hum of his motors rose to a whine and then to a scream. Freddie felt the great surge of power as they pulled away. All through the night they raced through the countryside until early next morning they drew gently into a siding.

'London!' said Fergus.

'Gosh!' breathed Freddie. 'What a wonderful run!'

While they were being unloaded another train stopped near them. 'Keep away from us!' called

59

Freddie. 'We don't want our fish ruined by the smell from petrol tankers or dust from grubby coal trucks!'

The others roared with laughter. 'Good old Freddie,' they chuckled. 'You are a real fish van!'

'I know!' grinned Freddie, sniffing the air happily.

Bertram the Bus

BERTRAM was a big green double-decker bus. He had a yellow stripe about his middle and doors which 'Sss-shed' and closed all by themselves – or at least, they shut with a little help from his driver. His seats were covered in bright red leather and his fittings were sparkling chromium plate and shiny cream plastic. Bertram was air-conditioned, which means that he could keep his passengers warm in winter and cool in summer and never, ever become stuffy. To ring his bell he had a long squashy rubber strip in his ceilings. Bertram thought that bell pushes were very old fashioned. He was a very new bus. He was also very vain.

When the driver from the factory where Bertram was born delivered him to the garage where he was to live, Bertram took one look at it, wrinkled his nose and said, 'Ugh! Do they expect me to live in this – this – cattle-shed? And just look at those buses! They're filthy!'

'Be quiet, Bertram,' said the factory driver. 'Remember your manners.'

'Manners!' snorted Bertram. 'I don't suppose that anyone here has ever even heard of manners.'

'What's all this?' asked a deep, rumbling voice.

'Ah! You must be the new bus. I'm the Inspector here and I can use a strapping fellow like you.' Then the Inspector walked thoughtfully around Bertram kicking each of his tyres in turn. 'Put him at the back of the shed, driver,' he said. 'Then come into the office and I will sign your forms.'

Bertram was speechless. He sat at the back of the garage and fumed!

Much later, the Inspector brought two workmen along to look at him. 'This is the new bus,' he said. 'He will be Number Ninety-Nine.'

'Number Ninety-Nine?' spluttered Bertram. 'I don't need a number. I've a perfectly good name – it's Bertram.'

'Oh! So you are Bertram are you?' said the Inspector.

'Yes,' said Bertram.

'Well now,' said the Inspector, 'that's very nice. Very nice indeed. But we have no time for fancy

63

names here. You will be "Ninety-Nine" and like it! And say "Sir" when you speak to me!' he snapped.

Bertram was so surprised that his bonnet popped open with shock. 'Y-y-yes sir!' he said weakly and stood there trembling with fright and anger while the workmen painted large '99's on his back and sides.

He was most curious when the workmen set up step ladders and planks beside him and climbed up to reach the yellow band around his middle.

'Please – what are you going to do now?' he asked politely, remembering his manners for once.

'Stick on your posters, of course,' they replied.

'My posters?' gasped Bertram. 'Posters on *me*?'

'All buses have posters,' they said. 'Now keep still, Ninety-Nine, or yours will all be crooked.'

'Stuck on posters? Posters stuck on with paste?'

'Of course. How else?'

'But it will simply ruin my paintwork,' groaned Bertram.

The workmen just laughed. 'You will soon stop worrying about your paintwork after you have been working in the rain and the mud for a while,' they said and stuck posters on each of his sides, his back

and – on his forehead! The poster on his forehead was about laundries and washing. Those on his sides shouted about peanuts and fizzy lemonade and the one on his back was rather rude and said that if anyone was able to read it, then he must be driving too close to Bertram for safety. Oh! The shame of it all!

When all the hot, tired, dirty buses came home after their hard day's work, they found Bertram sitting sulkily in his corner at the back of the shed.

'Look!' said Forty-Six to his friends. 'We have a new workmate.'

'Hello, Ninety-Nine,' they called cheerfully. 'Welcome to the garage.'

'Go away!' growled Bertram. 'You are old-fashioned, dirty buses and you all smell of stale oil. I am a very particular and modern bus and I certainly have no wish to join any family of yours.' With that, he closed his eyes very tightly because he believed, as some boys and girls do, that if he did he couldn't see or be seen – and he sulked.

'Have you ever heard anything like it?' asked Seventy-Eight. 'What a rude bus he is.'

'He wants nothing to do with any of us,' said Thirty-Six, 'so let's not have anything to do with him.'

'Let's send him to Coventry and never speak to him at all,' suggested Seventy-Eight.

'Yes, let's,' everyone shouted.

So that's exactly what they did. Poor Bertram sat in his corner and cried himself to sleep, while Seventy-Eight called him rude names and told everyone what an absolutely awful bus had come to live with them.

Next morning most of the other buses went out to work very early and Bertram was left alone in his dark corner until almost lunch time. Then the Inspector came into the shed with a driver and a conductor. 'This,' said the Inspector, 'is Ninety-Nine.' Then, turning to Bertram, he said, 'Now then, Ninety-Nine, you are an expensive new bus, we want some work out of you and no nonsense! Understand?'

'Yes,' said Bertram.

'Yes what?' snapped the Inspector.

'Y-yes – sir,' said Bertram.

'I should think so too. Now get on with it!' and away the Inspector stumped.

'Now then my lad,' said the driver. 'I'm Tom and I expect you to obey me without question.'

'Humph!' said Bertram.

'And I am Norman,' said the conductor, 'and

I shall expect you to do exactly as my bell tells you.'

'Humph!' said Bertram again.

'What an ignorant bus we have, to be sure,' said Norman.

'Indeed we have,' agreed Tom, 'but he had better behave, or I shall report him!'

Bertram was furious. Report him? They wouldn't dare!

Tom climbed into the driving seat and Norman stood on the platform. 'Ssssh!' went the door, 'Ting!' said the bell and away they went to the bus station in the centre of the town.

'Look out chaps!' called Forty-Seven to his friends when he saw Bertram coming. 'Here comes old toffee-nose!'

'Boo-oo-oo!' shouted all the other buses.

Bertram was so angry by the time he reached the market place that he wasn't thinking what he was doing at all. Suddenly, Tom trod hard on the brakes and it seemed that everyone was shouting at once. 'Look where you are going, stupid!' yelled Tom.

'Clumsy!' shouted Norman, grabbing at a shiny handrail, missing it and slithering down the whole length of the bus.

'Awkward bus!' shouted all the bus passengers at once.

But worst and most frightening of all, was a very loud 'Hey you!' from a very cross policeman who was marching straight towards Bertram and taking out a pencil and notebook from his tunic pocket as he came.

'Me?' quivered Bertram, his engine missing a beat.

'Who else?' asked the policeman. 'What's wrong with your eyesight? Do you need spectacles?'

'Certainly not!' spluttered Bertram. 'I am a very modern bus.'

'Modern you may be, but you are certainly not very bright.'

'What did I do?' asked Bertram, a little worried now.

'What *didn't* you do?' said the policeman. 'Why do you think I was standing in the middle of the road with my arm up? For fun?' he asked.

'I didn't even see you!' spluttered Bertram who was now beginning to realize that he had made some sort of mistake.

'When I put up my hand, it means that all the traffic must stop, including you! That is the law!'

71

'Yes,' said Bertram weakly.

'But you didn't stop. You didn't even see me,' said the policeman. 'Which means,' he continued, 'that you are a very careless bus and could have caused a nasty accident.'

'I'm sorry,' groaned Bertram.

'So you should be. But you committed an offence, so I shall have to make a note of your number.' And in his very best handwriting, he wrote, 'Number Ninety-Nine – a very careless bus,' in his little note book. What a disgrace!

For the rest of that day Bertram went back and forth along his route and was very quiet indeed. That night none of the other buses spoke to him at all and he cried himself to sleep once more while Seventy-Eight went on and on about careless buses who had their numbers taken.

Next morning, Bertram was awakened with a start. Tom and Norman were shaking him and shouting, 'Show a wheel, Ninety-Nine! It's time we were off!'

'But it's still dark,' protested Bertram.

'We know that,' said Norman and Tom.

'And it's raining too!' said Bertram. 'The roads will all be muddy and wet.'

'All the more reason for you to be out,' said

Norman. 'People really need buses on dark, nasty, wet mornings like this!'

'But my paint will be quite ruined, and I'll become as dirty as the rest,' moaned Bertram.

'It would be a miracle if you didn't,' said Tom. 'Now stop complaining and start work or the Inspector will report you.' That last remark did not improve Bertram's temper one scrap and he splashed angrily out of the garage and went grudgingly to work.

When it became light Bertram was able to see himself reflected in a shop window and a wetter and more bedraggled vehicle he had never seen. He looked awful. It almost broke his heart. But no matter how much he grumbled and protested, Tom drove him on and on. He refused to allow him to stop for a moment longer than necessary and Bertram became wetter and wetter, dirtier and dirtier.

Later that afternoon he found himself parked outside a large building in a part of the town he had never visited before. Tom and Norman sat inside him and smoked. 'Why are we waiting here?' muttered Bertram to himself. 'Standing around in this rain is enough to give a bus pneumonia.' He also began to wonder whatever this large building could be. At four o'clock he found out. It was a school! The doors opened, and out came more children than Bertram knew existed in the whole world. There were large ones, small ones, fat ones, thin ones, spotty ones, freckled ones, quiet ones, chatty ones. And most of them – or so it seemed to Bertram – piled into him. They sang and shouted,

bounced on his seats, opened his windows and shot tickets at each other with rubber bands. They covered his floor with sweet papers and trampled nasty pink chewing gum everywhere.

Bertram shook with temper. 'Why did you allow these hooligans in me?' he asked Tom and Norman. 'I'm being spoiled inside and out.'

'Stop complaining, Ninety-Nine,' said Norman. 'They pay their fares, so they are entitled to use you.'

The thought that he was being 'used' made Bertram angrier than ever. He seethed with rage.

He was glad when they reached the bus station, but they didn't stop there. They went off to wait outside another large building. Surely this wasn't another school! It wasn't. It was a factory. At half past five a hooter sounded, so suddenly and so loudly that Bertram almost jumped out of his tyres. A few moments later, lots of men with dirty, grimy hands, dirty, greasy overalls and dirty, clumpy boots came through the gates and climbed into him. They sat heavily down on his seats with a 'Flumph!' and most of them lit cigarettes. By the time he reached the bus station, Bertram's inside was thick with smoke and there were squashed cigarette ends all over his floor.

'I'm ruined,' groaned Bertram as he sat in his corner and wept, covered with mud and dirt, half full of sweet and chocolate wrappers, stuck up with chewing gum and cigarette ends. What a mess!

A little later, another bus crept up beside him. 'Don't cry, Ninety-Nine,' it said. 'We shall soon be cleaned.'

'Who are you?' sniffled Bertram.

'I'm Twenty-One,' said the other bus. 'You know, you really were a very rude and vain young bus and asked for all you got, but I don't agree with Seventy-Eight. He is spiteful. Some of us others think that you deserve a chance.'

'Do you?' asked Bertram, hopefully.

'Yes, but you will have to work very hard and prove that you deserve it,' said Twenty-One.

'I'll try,' said Bertram. 'I'll really try.'

Soon, some workmen came along and cleaned his inside, then they took him to another part of the depot where he was driven between great spinning brushes and squirted with water. 'Hee-hee!' giggled Bertram. 'It tickles!' but then he spluttered and spluttered as a stream of cold water hit him in the face.

For the next two weeks, Bertram worked without grumbling and the other buses began to talk to him

– except Seventy-Eight that is – and they winked at him with their lights as they passed. All went well until one Saturday afternoon Tom and some of the other drivers took their buses out on a special trip. They were all parked in a long line down one side of a narrow street but Bertram couldn't imagine what they were waiting for. Then from somewhere near at hand he heard a rumble and then he heard a roar. Whatever could it be? He knew! It was people, lots and lots of people and all of them shouting at once. They were at a football match – or they had been! Surging towards him, wearing red and white or yellow and black scarves and woollen caps, rattling rattles, blowing whistles came a great wave of people. Bertram was in a panic.

'Help!' he shouted. 'I'm off! We shall all be torn to pieces.' And away he went at breakneck speed.

'Stop!' shouted the Inspector who was there to keep the buses in order and to see that they all took their proper turns.

'Whoa!' said Tom.

'Steady boy!' said Norman.

But Bertram didn't stop, whoa or steady. He was too scared to listen. All he wanted to do was to get away from all these awful people. On and on he went and found himself on a road he didn't know.

He flashed past a sign which had a picture of a bridge and some numbers painted on it – but he didn't notice it. Tom and Norman saw it and shouted even louder for Bertram to stop, but it was too late. Suddenly he reached a railway bridge and he aimed to dive under it.

'CRUNCH!' Bertram had to stop now because he was stuck. It was a low bridge and the sign had been put there to warn him that a double-decker bus could not pass underneath.

Tom and Norman climbed out rather shakily. 'Here's a tidy mess,' they said. 'Now see what you have done. You're stuck!' Bertram didn't need to see that he was stuck. He could feel it! His upstairs front windows were shattered and the top front bit of his roof was rolled back just like a part-opened sardine tin. He had a headache too!

When the Inspector arrived with a breakdown truck he shouted and stormed at Bertram until his windscreen wipers rattled. 'You are the stupidest bus I ever knew!' he raged. 'Only cowards run away and you know what happens to them!'

'Yes, sir,' said Bertram in a very sorry voice. 'They get stuck!' The breakdown men had to let the air out of his tyres to release him and then he was towed away – backwards – right through the

middle of the town. Bertram had never felt so ashamed in all his life. Everyone laughed at him and Seventy-Eight sneered more than ever before.

For days Bertram crept about the town and tried hard not to be seen, which is very difficult when you are a bus and people are looking for you. Then, one day, Bertram was standing near the school as usual and waiting for the children to come out. He dreaded it. 'Cowardy, cowardy custard,' they would shout. 'Ninety-Nine's a scaredy cat!' It was awful. Suddenly, Bertram heard the sound of a motor hooter. It went on and on as though it were stuck. But no, it wasn't a stuck hooter. It was a danger hooter, a warning hooter. Then Bertram saw the reason for it. There was a runaway lorry careering down the hill and it was heading straight for all the children who were just coming out of school!

Bertram didn't stop to think. He didn't wait for Tom to tell him what to do. He ran into the road at the bottom of the hill, right in front of the run-away lorry. Then he closed his eyes, clenched his clutch, gritted his gears – and waited.

'Whomp!' The lorry hit him right in the stomach and knocked all the breath out of him. His side was caved in, almost all his downstairs windows were broken, some of his seats were ripped and buckled and one of his posters was torn. Bertram shook and quivered and a puddle of oil formed somewhere underneath.

For the second time in a short while, Bertram was towed through the town. But this time it was different. The Inspector himself drove the breakdown lorry. A police car led the way and all the children walked beside him cheering. They shouted and called out to everyone and told them what Bertram had done. 'Good old Ninety-Nine,' they said.

Back in the garage, the Inspector stroked his battered side and said, 'Good lad, Bertram!'

'What did you say?' asked Bertram.

'I said, "Good lad"!'

'Yes, I know. But you said something else. You called me Bertram.'

'That's right. It's your name isn't it?'

'Yes, sir,' said Bertram.

'And it does sound better than just Ninety-Nine doesn't it?'

'Yes, sir.'

'Well, because you are a very brave bus, I think that we can stretch a point, don't you?'

'Can we?' asked Bertram.

'Yes, but we shall call you "Bertie". It sounds much more friendly, don't you think?

'Oh, sir. Yes please,' said Bertram – or Bertie.

Bertie was sent off to the factory to be repaired, and guess what? On his bonnet, in neat gold letters edged with black, was written for all to see 'BERTIE V.B.B.'

'Please, sir,' Bertie asked the Inspector, 'what does V.B.B. mean?'

'Very Brave Bus, of course,' he replied.

Bertie became the most popular bus in the town and in the garage. He was happy for the first time in his life. The children loved him and he looked forward to seeing them every day. He did his job better than any bus ever had. He never grumbled. He was liked. He was popular. He belonged.

As they settled down to sleep on his return from the factory, Twenty-One whispered, 'Good night, Bertie. Pleasant dreams.'

'Good night, Twenty-One,' said Bertie.

'Please, Bertie,' said Twenty-One, 'call me Daisy! That's my name.'

'Good night, Daisy,' said Bertie. 'I'm so glad that I took your advice.'

Vernon the Vacuum Cleaner

VERNON was disgusted! He sat in his cardboard box and fumed. It seemed to him that he had been shut in there for years. Corrugated cardboard boxes are all very well for some people and are ideal to pack things in when they come newly made from factories but they are dreadful if it's you shut up in there. They are very dark, cramped and uncomfortable things to be shut in. Vernon was standing on his head inside his corrugated cardboard box. That is why he was so disgusted. That, and the fact that he couldn't see out. You could say that Vernon had been born nosey for after all he was a vacuum cleaner, though he didn't know that yet.

He stood there, cramped and upside down for several more days until quite suddenly he felt himself picked up and carried to goodness knows where. He was put down with a thump which

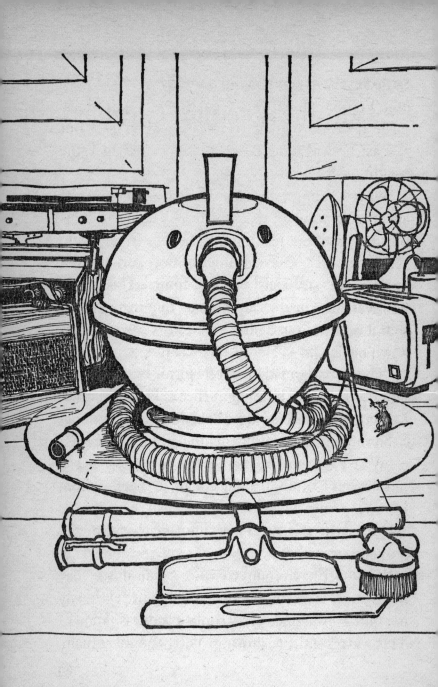

rattled every nut and bolt in his body. 'Oof! Ouch!' said Vernon. 'A fat lot of good it is being newly made if they are going to treat me like that!' But at least he was lying down now and that took the weight off his head.

'Now I suppose that I shall just lie here until I am too old to be of use,' moaned Vernon to himself, but within a few minutes he was lifted again. 'Here we go!' said Vernon as he found himself once more standing on his head. This time, however, he heard a ripping, rending, tearing sound and he was hauled out of his box and put down on the floor. He was in a shop.

'That's better!' said Vernon as he gazed about him. 'It's good to be out and not before time either. I couldn't be seen in there!' Have I mentioned that Vernon was vain as well as inquisitive? He was!

'Where do you want this, Mr Sparkes?' asked the shop assistant who had just lifted Vernon from his box.

'Put it in the centre of the window display,' replied the manager, 'It's the very latest model.'

'This? It?' Vernon snorted. 'I suppose they mean me!' Then he sniffed, 'These are certainly not the most respectful people I have ever met.' This wasn't really surprising. You don't meet many

89

people when you are newly made and fresh from
the factory and have spent all your life in a corrugated cardboard box.

At that moment the shop assistant lifted Vernon
and placed him in the middle of a shiny, flat, round
plate-thing which stood in the centre of the window
display and arranged all his parts and pieces beside
him. 'This is much better,' said Vernon grandly.
'At last they have realized just how important I
am!' And indeed, people were already looking at
him through the window. Well, that's what Vernon
thought, but they were actually looking at electric
fires, toasters, mixers, radios, record players, tape-
recorders, hair-dryers and many other things.
Vernon was much too vain to think of anything
except himself and so didn't notice any of the other
things.

'I've done that, Mr Sparkes,' called out the shop
assistant, 'and laid out all the accessories.'

'Good,' replied the manager. 'Put a showcard
and a price ticket on it and that will be all for now.'

'Right!' said the assistant, propping a large card
against Vernon's side and putting another, with
numbers on it, in front of him. Vernon wished that
he could see what was written on those cards but
it was quite impossible to read something propped

against his side or right underneath his nose with its back towards him. He didn't worry about it for very long, however, for he was far too busy being the centre of attraction, raised up above all the other things in the window and with lights shining upon him.

Then without warning, the platform on which Vernon was standing began slowly turning round. 'I suppose that they want to show my better side,' he purred. But he was turning right round and round and round, without stopping! It was quite fun at first, but then Vernon became rather annoyed. 'This is quite ridiculous!' he pouted. 'They should make up their minds which way they want me facing and then just leave me alone.' But of course, as you will know by now, Vernon was on one of those turntable things which are often used in shop windows and are meant to go round and round for ever and almost ever. Vernon felt giddy and then he began to feel sick. 'This is going too far!' he shouted. 'Stop it. Stop it, do!' But the turntable wasn't going to stop. It just kept going round and round and Vernon went with it!

That night, when the shop was closed, when no people passed in the street outside and when Vernon was becoming used to revolving, he heard a little scuffle and saw a little grey-brown some-thing in the bottom of the window. When he had revolved again he saw that it had moved and noticed that it had a long tail. When he came round yet again, he saw that it was a mouse!

'Good evening!' said the mouse. He seemed to be a reasonably well-mannered little creature, so when Vernon passed the next time he replied, 'Good evening, Mouse.'

Next time round Mouse asked, 'Who are you?' and the time after that, Vernon replied, 'I'm Vernon.'

'I say,' said Mouse, 'would you please stand still for a moment. It really is awfully difficult to hold a conversation with someone who keeps going round and round.' (Vernon had been round twice whilst Mouse said that!)

'I can't,' complained Vernon. 'I'm not to blame. It's the thing I'm standing on. It won't stop!'

'Then I shall come round with you,' said Mouse, hopping on to the turntable. 'That's better,' he said. 'Now we can talk.'

Vernon noticed that Mouse was reading the card propped against his side. At last he could find out what had been written about him.

'Excuse me, Mouse,' he said quite politely (he

could be most polite when he wanted something), 'would you mind telling me what it says on that card? I can't see it from here.'

'Certainly,' said Mouse. 'It says, "Presenting the Latest Five Star Vacuum Cleaner".'

'Thank you,' said Vernon. 'So that's what I am – a vacuum cleaner!'

'So it says there,' said Mouse.

'I wonder what I'm for?' mused Vernon.

'I haven't the faintest idea,' replied Mouse, who hadn't been meant to hear. 'But you have an awfully long nose to do it with. Doesn't it ever get tangled up or trapped in anything?'

'I'll thank you to keep your remarks to yourself,' snorted Vernon. 'My nose is no business of yours!'

'It could be useful for sniffing around corners,' suggested Mouse, but Vernon was not amused.

'I could make remarks about your tail too,' he threatened.

'You should see your own,' Mouse giggled. 'It is so long that it has had to be coiled up and tied round the middle.'

'Enough!' snapped Vernon. 'What I would like to know is, what exactly do I do?'

'And I said,' replied Mouse, 'that I hadn't the faintest idea.'

'What does "Vacuum Cleaner" mean?' asked Vernon.

'Well,' said Mouse, 'if you clean something, you – er – make it clean, get rid of the dust and dirt. You clean it!'

Vernon was most annoyed. 'Indeed, I shall do no such thing. Getting rid of dust and dirt. Ugh! It can't be that. What about the other word?'

'Vacuum?' asked Mouse.

'Yes.'

'Oh, I know what that means,' Mouse confided. 'A vacuum is a hole full of nothing!'

'That's it!' said Vernon happily. 'A vacuum cleaner – a nothing cleaner – I clean nothing!'

'What are you for then?'

'Oh, just to sit around and be shown off. Exactly what I am doing now!'

'Seems a bit queer to me,' said Mouse doubtfully.

'What about the other card?' asked Vernon. 'What does that say?'

'It says,' said Mouse, '23 dot 99 Complete.'

'Hmph!' said Vernon.

'I suppose,' mused Mouse, 'that "Complete" means you and your bits.'

'Bits!' exploded Vernon. 'BITS! I don't have

bits. I have "Accessories", the assistant said so.'

'Pardon me,' sniffed Mouse.

'Granted,' said Vernon. 'But what's 23 dot 99?'

'I think that's money,' said Mouse.

'What's money?'

'It's pieces of coloured paper and shiny round metal things that people keep giving away,' said Mouse.

'Is that all?' gasped Vernon.

'Well they are valuable and I would think that a brand new something bought by someone who wanted to clean nothing was expensive at any price.'

'Quite,' said Vernon.

Mouse wished Vernon good night and went off to the place where the manager hid his chocolate biscuits, while Vernon spun himself to sleep.

Some days later, Vernon was taken from his window and repacked into his cardboard carton. He had been sold! His new owner seemed nice enough from what he saw of her as he was whisked past, but he was most disappointed at not seeing the 23 dot 99 handed over for him. He would have liked to have seen what it was.

'I suppose,' he thought to himself, 'that I shall

be placed in the middle of my owner's window for all her friends to come and admire. How very nice!' But there was a surprise in store for him. He wasn't placed in a window. He was shut in a cupboard instead.

'Good gracious!' said Vernon. 'People have some very odd ideas.'

'Hello!' said a voice. 'Who are you? I'm Broom.'

'Vernon,' replied Vernon, rudely.

'Hello, Vernon,' said another voice. 'I am Carpet Brush and I'm very pleased to meet you.'

'So am I,' said Mop.

'So am I,' said Dustpan, and Sweeper, and Duster.

Vernon pricked up his ears. These scruffy old objects were pleased to see him! This was most unexpected. Perhaps he was famous. He looked down upon them from his place on the shelf. 'I am so glad that you have come,' said Carpet Brush. 'We have needed a vacuum cleaner here for a long time.'

'Indeed,' said Vernon, feeling quite flattered now.

'Yes,' said Broom. 'Carpet Brush is going quite bald with the work and the worry in this place and I have a few grey bristles myself.'

'I quite agree,' said Duster. 'I'm threadbare with it all.'

'It's worse than ever now,' chipped in Sweeper, 'with two grown ups, four children, a cat, a dog and a budgie dropping bits all over the place.'

'We do need a vacuum cleaner,' said Mop.

Dustpan agreed, 'Quite so,' he said. 'All the dirt and dust, crumbs, animal hair, feathers and bird-seed are getting me down. We most certainly need you, Vernon!'

'It sounds a horrid place to be in,' growled Vernon, a little worried now. 'And I cannot see what so much dust and dirt has to do with your needing me.'

'Can't you?' said Dustpan and Carpet Brush together.

'We need you to suck up all the dust and fluff,' said Sweeper. 'Why else?'

'Me, suck up dust and dirt?' gasped Vernon. 'What a horrid suggestion. I am a vacuum cleaner you know.'

'We know that,' said Broom. 'That's why you have such a long bendy nose. It's fine for sucking up dirt.'

'What an absolutely revolting suggestion,'

snorted Vernon. 'You are all most disgusting and uncouth.'

'Nothing of the kind,' said Duster, crossly. 'Whatever are vacuum cleaners for, if not to suck up dirt? Tell me that!'

Vernon carefully explained what a vacuum cleaner was and did (at least, he gave his own and Mouse's version of what they thought it was). The others roared with laughter. They laughed and laughed until Broom fell off his clip with a clunk, but even that didn't stop him laughing.

Later that day, Vernon was taken from the cupboard. 'Oh!' he thought. 'Now we shall see who was right.'

His new owner knew all about vacuum cleaners. She unwound his cable, plugged it in to a power point and switched it on. Vernon felt something prickle and tickle inside him before the whirr and hum of his motor almost scared him clean out of his casing. 'I do things!' he said in astonishment. His owner led him by the nose and he found that he had begun to suck things up!

'Pooh!' he said as his nose filled with dust, but soon he was thoroughly enjoying himself. He sucked up dust, fluff, hairs, pins, birdseed, feathers and a whole host of other things. Then he began to hunt. He hunted in the curtains, he hunted in, on and under the chairs. Vernon went absolutely everywhere, and wherever he went, three little boys and a girl went too. The little girl rode on his back and everyone cheered.

Halfway down the stairs, Vernon swallowed a sweet. He didn't really like it, he didn't particularly want it. It was a sweet the little girl had dropped. It was a very sticky sweet and it stuck at the top of his nose. 'By node id blocked,' snuffled Vernon as the dust, hair, grit, fluff and old birdseed stuck at the top of his nose.

'Something is wrong with him, Mummy,' said the little girl. 'He can't suck.'

'He's blocked, I expect,' said her mother as she switched him off. 'Something of yours he picked up, I shouldn't wonder,' she told the boys.

'It couldn't be anything of ours,' they said.

Vernon's nose was soon unblocked and everyone was shown what had caused all the trouble and since Vernon was such an expensive vacuum cleaner the children promised never to leave anything around which might get stuck in Vernon and hurt him.

By this time Vernon had a slight feeling of

indigestion, so he whistled to be emptied. 'Pe-ee-eep!' Just like that.

'However does he know when he is full?' asked the children.

'How do you?' laughed their mother. 'This is a very clever vacuum cleaner,' she said and everyone agreed.

Back in the cupboard, Vernon was greeted with shouts and cheers.

'Good old Vernon,' everyone shouted. 'You have cleaned the whole lot!'

'It was nothing,' said Vernon. 'Nothing at all. I said that it was all quite easy!'

'You said nothing of the s . . .!' began Broom, but he stopped when he saw Vernon grinning at him. And they all roared with laughter.

Cuthbert the Caravan

M R ARBUTHNOT BRAITH-
WAITE sat in his shirt sleeves and drank cool fizzy
lemonade. 'My word!' he said, 'it's hot this
morning, but it should be good for trade.'

Mr Braithwaite's office was a little wooden shed
at the entrance to a large field which lay beside the
London Road. Over the white-painted wooden
gate was a big sign which read, 'CARA-HOMES
LIMITED. CARAVANS FOR SALE OR HIRE' in
large red capital letters and then in smaller letters,
'Arbuthnot Braithwaite, Prop.'

The field was full of caravans of every size and
shape, all looking very smart. Mr Braithwaite
boasted that he was able to supply every possible
kind of caravan – he had collapsible caravans which
folded neatly away into tiny trailers, caravans with
two beds or berths, three berths, four berths and
some with as many as six. He had caravans with

Cuthbert the Caravan

fully fitted kitchens and gas cookers and some with only little paraffin stoves. He had a tinker's caravan which was nothing more than a big tarpaulin thrown over a frame on a flat wooden cart and a real gypsy caravan gaily painted with pretty patterns

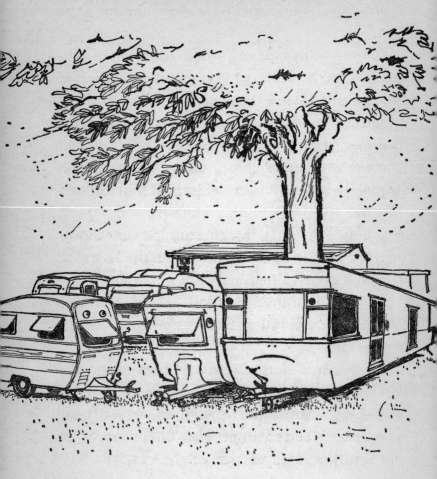

and flowers. But his pride and joy was the enormous white caravan parked under a shady chestnut tree at the far end of his showground. 'It's a beauty!' sighed Mr Braithwaite each time he looked at it, 'I shall be sorry to see it go, but I shall have to sell it one day and I could certainly do with the cash.'

The big white caravan, whose name was Cuthbert, sat in the shade of the chestnut and smiled smugly to himself. 'What a fine fellow I am!' he repeated over and over to himself. Mr Braithwaite had washed him and dusted him as usual that morning and since then Cuthbert had noticed him looking his way several times. It made him feel very pleased.

'Phew! I'm hot!' gasped the little green two-berthed caravan who stood at Cuthbert's right. 'The sun is blistering my roof.'

'So am I,' said the blue four-berth on Cuthbert's left. 'Some people have all the luck. I wish we were in the shade.'

'It isn't luck,' said Cuthbert. 'I need taking care of, I'm very special.'

'I can't see what's so special about you,' said Two-berth. 'You're no better than the rest of us, you're just a bit bigger, that's all!'

Cuthbert almost exploded with anger. 'I'm nothing like you,' he snorted, 'and I'm certainly not a caravan!'

'If you're not a caravan, then what are you?' asked Two-berth. 'I can't see anything to make such a fuss about.'

'Oh can't you!' said Cuthbert. 'You'll see if you look at the card in my window that I'm a mobile home, not a caravan!'

'Caravan, mobile home, what's the difference? We are really all the same.'

'I'll tell you what's the difference,' stormed Cuthbert, 'I'm not like you lot at all. Take a look at me. Go on! I'm not a shed on wheels!'

'We've looked at you already,' said Two-berth. 'You're so large that we can't help seeing you.'

'There's no need for rudeness,' snapped Cuthbert. 'Tell me, Two-berth, what's inside you?'

'Two beds, a cupboard, a table and a wardrobe, a stove, a gas cooker and a sink,' came the reply.

'What about you, Four-berth? What do you have inside?'

'Much the same as Two-berth,' said Four-berth. 'But I have more beds and cupboards and can be divided into two.'

'Quite so. Now I'll tell you what I have inside

me,' said Cuthbert, 'I have two bedrooms, a dining room, a kitchen and a bathroom and I'm fully furnished throughout. I have magnificent curtains and fitted carpets and two television sets. I also have, as you'll have noticed, a balcony, a bay window, a front porch and a letter box on my door. That's the difference between us. You are just ordinary caravans, and *I* am a mobile home.'

'You're not really!' said Two-berth.

Cuthbert was astonished. 'What did you say?' he said.

'I said, you're not really mobile,' said Two-berth. 'You're stationary and have been for some time. And anyway, not even you can move around by yourself!'

'And you're not really a home without people,' added Four-berth, 'and who'd want to live in you?'

Cuthbert had never felt so insulted in all his life.

Later that afternoon a little red sports car drew up beside the office and a young lady and gentleman climbed out. Mr Braithwaite greeted them warmly and they walked over towards Cuthbert. 'Here come some admirers,' thought Cuthbert. 'They are certain to fall for me.' But they didn't even look at him. They bought little Two-berth and took him away.

'Good-bye, everyone,' called Two-berth. 'Perhaps I shall see you again one day.'

'Good-bye, Two-berth,' they shouted, but Cuthbert snorted, 'Humph! Stupid people! Fancy wanting a thing like that!'

Then a large, smart black car stopped at the office and out of it stepped a father, a mother and two children.

'Ah!' said Cuthbert, 'this is more like it. They are bound to be interested in me.' But they weren't! They bought Four-berth and then they towed him away.

Much later, a dirty old blue lorry rattled in through the gateway and a little fat man clambered out. 'Looks like a junk man,' thought Cuthbert, 'called to see if Mr Braithwaite has any scrap.' But he was wrong. Before Cuthbert realized what was happening, this man had bought him. Cuthbert thought he would never live down being towed out by a dirty old lorry and in full view of those common caravans.

'Rags and bones!' they shouted and jeered. 'Have fun on the scrap heap.'

'Hey, lorry!' snarled Cuthbert as they bounced out on to the main road, 'Be careful! Don't bang me about like that!'

'Be quiet, you great lumbering van!' ordered the lorry. 'I'm not going to enjoy this either. I'd rather carry a load of old scrap!'

For the next two hours Cuthbert raged and fumed to himself and then as they climbed a very steep hill he was choked in a cloud of black oily smoke. 'Ugh!' he spluttered. 'The exhaust from this dirty old lorry will absolutely ruin my paint,' and he tried to swing to one side to avoid it.

'Be-ee-eep!' screamed a coach as it rushed past in the opposite direction. 'Do you want to get flattened, you stupid thing?'

'Stop messing about!' snarled the blue lorry. 'I'm having trouble enough as it is!'

'Pah!' said Cuthbert, moving back into line. But the fumes were still annoying him, so he tried swinging out on the other side. There would be no coaches to shout at him there.

'Get back!' yelled the old lorry. 'You'll tip yourself into that ditch!' But his warning came too late.

Cuthbert ran on to the grass verge and stopped suddenly against some very prickly bushes, with his near-side wheels in several inches of smelly, muddy water. 'Oh dear!' he said, 'I think I've sprained my towing bar!'

With some difficulty the little fat man unhitched him from the lorry. 'Here's a fine mess,' he said. 'I'll need help to pull you out of there. I can't manage it all by myself!'

So Cuthbert spent that night and the following morning in a ditch until the little fat man arrived with a tractor to haul him out.

They were trundling slowly down the road with Cuthbert dripping mud everywhere when they were overtaken by the red sports car with little Two-berth bowling along happily behind. 'Hello

there, Cuthbert!' he called, 'Having trouble? We're off to the sea for two weeks!'

'Humph!' said Cuthbert.

Late that afternoon he was towed into a muddy field full of lorries, old buses, coaches, tractors and people hustling and bustling about.

'Where am I?' he wailed.

'In a fairground, of course,' replied his neighbour, a large red caravan. 'You must be dull if you didn't know that.'

'A fairground!' spluttered Cuthbert. 'What a terrible place to be.'

'No it isn't!' said the red caravan. 'It's fun when you get used to it, you'll see.'

'Never!' said Cuthbert. 'The noise will drive me mad.' He sniffed. 'What's that smell? It's like cooking!'

'It is,' said the red caravan. 'It's me!'

'You?'

'Well, not me exactly. It's hot dogs actually.'

'Whatever are hot dogs?' asked Cuthbert with a puzzled frown.

'Sausages! I'm a hot dog stall,' said the red caravan. 'We cook and sell sausages you see.'

'How revolting!' said Cuthbert. 'I'm a mobile home.'

'Congratulations,' said the red caravan. 'Your
neighbour on the other side is a fish bar. He sells
jellied eels and shell fish!'

Cuthbert groaned. What a place!

The little fat man who owned Cuthbert and the

old blue lorry also owned a roundabout with painted wooden horses, and all through the summer they travelled from fairground to fairground. Cuthbert grew grubbier and grubbier, muddier and muddier, and more and more scratched and down at heel until he became dreadfully depressed. This was no life for a splendid modern mobile home.

One day he found himself parked on the edge of a pleasant green meadow, next to a huge yellow caravan which he had never seen before. The field he was in sloped down gently to a beach and beyond that was the sea. 'What wouldn't I give to be down there on that lovely golden sand,' he thought. 'Or to be washed by that sparkling sea.'

'What did you say?' asked his enormous neighbour.

'Oh! Nothing much,' said Cuthbert. 'You're big! What's inside you?' There was a terrible roar from inside the yellow van and he jumped on his chassis with shock.

'Lions!' said his new neighbour, and there was another terrifying roar. Cuthbert jumped even more violently, and then he felt himself moving forward rolling across the field.

When the little fat man saw him Cuthbert was half-way down to the beach and gathering speed.

'Stop! Come back!' he yelled, but Cuthbert couldn't have stopped if he'd tried. He was heading faster and faster for the sea. He was on the shingle

now. Then, 'Whee-ee-ee!' he shouted as he slithered across the sand.

The little fat man was joined by a whole crowd of people and they all raced down to the beach, shouting and waving as they ran, but Cuthbert wasn't bothered. He had almost reached the sea. 'I'm going to have a paddle!' he shouted, 'I'm going to have a bathe!'

Whoosh! a large wave struck him. Whoosh, whoosh! so did another two. 'Brrr! It's cold!' he shivered, 'I don't think I'll stay in too long!'

Whoosh! The next wave lifted him off his wheels and he soon found himself floating and heading out to sea.

The little fat man was up to his waist in water. 'Come back here this minute!' he ordered and Cuthbert wished that he could.

A very cold and very scared mobile home floated out on the tide. Up and down, up and down he bobbed until he began to feel quite ill.

'Ship ahoy!' shouted the look-out on the fishing boat *Mary Ann*. 'Ship on the port beam! No it isn't!' he said when he looked again. 'It's a big white caravan!'

'Don't be ridiculous!' scoffed the Captain. 'There are no caravans at sea!'

'Take a look for yourself then!' said the look-out and handed the Captain his telescope.

'Shiver my timbers! You're right, look-out,' he said. 'Where do you think that that came from?'

The coastguard could hardly believe his ears

when he received the radio message. 'A caravan adrift in the channel?' he said. 'You must be pulling my leg!'

When he rang the lifeboat station, they thought he had gone quite mad. 'It's the lonely life he leads

up there on the cliff-top,' said the coxswain. 'He's beginning to see funny things!'

'No, I'm not!' protested the coastguard. 'The message came from the Captain of the *Mary Ann*!'

So they launched the lifeboat and went out to see for themselves.

Cuthbert was feeling dreadfully poorly when the lifeboat came and took him in tow. 'A fine thing!' grumbled the Coxswain, 'Having to come out and rescue a drifting caravan! We'll just have to beach you and your owner must do the rest.'

Cuthbert didn't mind what happened so long as there was firm, dry ground under his wheels again and he didn't make any protest when the little fat man brought along two large elephants to help haul him up the beach. 'Here's a fine kettle of fish,' he muttered. 'Our very first day with the circus, and you have to put out to sea! Never mind though,' he added, 'all's well that ends well and the publicity will be good for trade!'

Next morning Mr Braithwaite was reading his morning paper in his office when he saw a photograph of Cuthbert heading out to sea. 'Good

gracious!' he exclaimed. 'I'm sure that's one of mine!' So he painted another large notice and hung it on his gate. It's still there. 'SEA-GOING CARAVANS A SPECIALITY' it reads.

We hope you have enjoyed this book.
There are many more Young Puffins to
choose from, and some of them
are described on the following pages.

BEL THE GIANT AND OTHER STORIES
Helen Clare

More imaginative and charming stories for four and
five year olds, told by the author of *Five Dolls in a House.*

THE DOLLS' HOUSE
Rumer Godden

Mr and Mrs Plantaganet and their family were very
happy in their antique doll's house, until Marchpane the
elegant, selfish china doll moved in with them and acted
as if she owned the place.

HOW THE WHALE BECAME AND OTHER STORIES
Ted Hughes

Eleven stories, beautifully told by one of our leading
younger poets.

ALBERT
Alison Jezard

The adventures of a nice cheerful bachelor bear who
lives in the East End of London.

DEAR TEDDY ROBINSON
ABOUT TEDDY ROBINSON
TEDDY ROBINSON HIMSELF
KEEPING UP WITH TEDDY ROBINSON
Joan G. Robinson

Teddy Robinson was Deborah's teddy bear and such
a very nice, friendly, cuddly bear that he went
everywhere with her – and had even more
adventures than she did.

CLEVER POLLY AND THE STUPID WOLF
POLLY AND THE WOLF AGAIN
Catherine Storr

Clever Polly manages to think of lots of good ideas to
stop the stupid wolf from eating her.

GOBBOLINO, THE WITCH'S CAT
Ursula Moray Williams

Gobbolino's mother was ashamed of him because his
eyes were blue instead of green, and he wanted to be
loved instead of learning spells. So he went in search of
a friendly kitchen.

THE HAPPY ORPHELINE
Natalie Savage Carlson

The twenty little orphaned girls who live with Madame
Flattot are terrified of being adopted because they are
so happy.

A BROTHER FOR THE ORPHELINES
Natalie Savage Carlson

Sequel to *The Happy Orpheline*. Josine, the smallest of all
the orphans, finds a baby left on the doorstep. But he is
a *boy*. So the orphans plot and worry to find a way
to keep him.

A GIFT FROM WINKLESEA
Helen Cresswell

Dan and Mary buy a beautiful stone like an egg as a
present for their mother – and then it hatches out, into
the oddest animal they ever saw.

LITTLE BEAR'S FEATHER
and RUN FOR HOME
Evelyn Davies

Two separate stories on similar themes: Little Bear is a Red Indian Chief's son, Matthew the child of English settlers in Red Indian territory. They both have a dream and both find they must be brave in an unexpected way to realize it.

THE TEN TALES OF SHELLOVER
Ruth Ainsworth

Shellover the tortoise tells one story for each of the creatures in Mrs Candy's garden.

ROBIN
Catherine Storr

Robin was the youngest of three, and hated it. And then he discovered the shell called the Freedom of the Seas – and became the wonder of his family.

MISS HAPPINESS AND MISS FLOWER
Rumer Godden

Nona was lonely far away from her home in India, and the two dainty Japanese dolls, Miss Happiness and Miss Flower, were lonely too. But once Nona started building them a proper Japanese house they all felt better.

MAGIC IN MY POCKET
Alison Uttley

A selection of short stories by this well-loved author, especially good for five and six year olds.

THE SECRET SHOEMAKERS
James Reeves

A dozen of Grimms' least-known fairy tales retold
with all a poet's magic, and illustrated sympathetically
by Edward Ardizzone.

TALES FROM THE END COTTAGE
MORE TALES FROM THE END COTTAGE
Eileen Bell

Two tabby cats and a Peke live with Mrs Apple in a
Northamptonshire cottage. They quarrel, have
adventures and entertain dangerous strangers. A new
author with a special talent for writing about animals.
For reading aloud to 5 and over, private reading 7
plus. (*Originals*)

GEORGE
Agnes Sligh Turnbull

George was good at arithmetic, and housekeeping, and
at keeping children happy and well behaved. The pity
of it was that he was a rabbit so Mr Weaver didn't
believe in him. Splendid for six year olds and over.

THE YOUNG PUFFIN BOOK OF VERSE
Barbara Ireson

A deluge of poems about such fascinating subjects as
birds and balloons, mice and moonshine, farmers and
frogs, pigeons and pirates, especially chosen to please
young people of four to eight. (*Original*)